Family in Progress
by Ryia Delgado

I would like to dedicate this book to all my friends and my family. Thank you for always being there for me and giving me so much support. I love you all.

Beginnings

Samantha's POV

My mom passed away when I was two. After she died it was just my dad and me. He raised me for four years before he married Sophie, my step mom. Sophie got pregnant a few years later and had my brother Kyle. The relationship between Sophie and I was unique and wonderful and she was always so understanding when I talked about my real mom; they actually knew each other a few years in high school before she left for New York and later on married my dad, and had me.

When I was in my junior year of high school, I got pregnant with my son, Micah. I was just 17 at the time and before I got the chance to tell Micah's father anything about it, he dumped me. I dropped out two weeks after I found out. My Dad and Sophie supported me through the whole process. I was lucky enough to finish school online and got my diploma and took a few classes at the college just out of town.

After Micah's first birthday, Sophie offered me a job at her publishing house as a paid intern. I've been working there ever since, and I get full time day care for Micah, as well.

There was a reason I decided not to tell his father about him. After countless talks with Sophie, who always encouraged me to at least call him when I was pregnant, I never had the courage to. I figured he would just blow it off and tell me it wasn't his or something. I don't think I could handle that kind of humiliation. Even though I was one hundred percent sure who his father was, I just didn't want to have some huge custody battle or have to go through DNA testing to prove myself. My dad actually supported me when I told him all my worries about that, but I think he just didn't want to add more stress to my already full plate.

I love my life just the way it is, having a tiny human to hold in my arms at night is priceless and to have such a loving family is simply wonderful. From the outside people might say I have the perfect life, but that is so far from the truth. I love my Dad, and Sophie is an amazing mother who brought my brother into our lives. I couldn't have asked for better people to support me in my life, and having Micah has brought new wonders to all of our lives. My only wish is that he could have a dad in his life, but I know that could never happen.

It's four o'clock and I'm awakened by Micah sneaking into my bed. He wraps his little arm around my shoulder and falls back asleep quietly. I do the same and before I know it I'm awakened two hours later by my alarm clock. I get up and do my usual morning routine and run the bath for Micah, I undress and bathe him.

"Mama,"

"Yeah, buddy?"

"Do you work today?" I pick him up out of the tub after rinsing out the soap in his hair and wrap his towel around him.

"Yeah honey, mommy works today."

I kiss him on the head before I sit him on the counter to brush his teeth. Having a three year old ask questions like that sucks. I wish I could stay home with him all day every day. I pick him up off the counter and we walk back to our room. I grab a pair of jeans from his clothing drawer and he picks out his own shirt. I pull his blue jeans over his legs and he pulls his shirt over his head. I slip his socks and shoes on and turn the TV on for him to watch as I start getting myself ready.

I lay out my skirt and blouse for the day on the bed and quickly fix my hair and do my makeup. I brush my teeth and then begin to get dressed and slip my shoes on. I grab Micah's bag, my purse, and pick him up to head upstairs.

Sophie has breakfast on the table for everyone when we reach the top of the stairs. I sit Micah in a chair and serve him some food on his plate before I go to wake up my brother.

Surprises

Louis POV

Every morning since my first day of college had been simple; I'd wake up, take a shower, get dressed, and make breakfast. But today is different. Today I start my new job and I'm honestly terrified. I thought I tanked my interview with Mrs. Foreman or, as she requested me to call her, Sophie. After I graduated CSU at the top of my class, my mom begged me to move back home and apply at this new publishing office and to my surprise I actually got the job.

I grab my car keys and head out the door, quickly stopping by a small coffee shop on my way to work. All those years of school and I'm finally done and moving on to this. I can't believe I was hired as manager.

When I get to the office I have a note on my desk, I read it over and see that it's from my boss' secretary: "Hi Louis, Mrs. Foreman is out of town for the week. She has asked that you forgive her for not giving you proper instructions on your work schedule and duties for your first day. She asks that you simply keep an eye on the interns in your division, as there are only 12. She will give you her instructions when she returns next Monday. Thanks for understanding, and welcome."

I take a seat in my new office chair and type in the computer pass code I received this morning. After filling out a few credentials on the computer and finishing some paper work I decide to get some coffee in the break room and check up on everyone. Outside of my office are cubicles - which I assume is where the interns work, I look around, studying everyone, when I recognize a familiar face; I could be wrong, but that looks like Samantha, my old high school girlfriend. She leaves from her desk after answering a phone call, and I duck behind a cubicle. Why am I hiding?

I walk to the break room after she gets on the elevator. Where is she going? There are a few people in here on their lunch hour, I assume. I grab a doughnut and pour myself a cup of coffee. I sit down and introduce myself to a few of them, I find out that two of them are interns on my floor and the others are from the division on the floor above. As I'm making chit chat with them I see Sam again, getting off the elevator. I walk back to my office casually, trying not to make eye contact and just as I enter my office she looks my way. Did she see me? Why do I keep doing this? Stop it, Louis! She's just a girl you used to date and now you happen to be her boss, kind of. I tend to the rest of my work and finish filling out some papers before the work day is finally over. All the interns are gone so I pack up my unneeded briefcase and head to the elevator.

Samantha's POV

I finish editing the manuscript for the day and I pack my stuff up to leave. Why am I always the last one to leave the office? I knock over a few papers on my desk, so I crawl under my desk to grab them when I hear a door close. Who could that be? I wonder.

I quickly put the papers back on my desk, straightening them out, when I turn to see the person I was hoping not to run into today. His expression mirrors my own I'm sure; I grab my purse and my phone off my desk as he decides to speak up.

"Samantha, I thought - I mean I could tell, but I didn't. Umm… hi." He scratches the back of his head and does that weird thing I always hated, with his feet.

"Louis, hi, so I see you're the new manager here."

"Yeah, I just got out of college and my mom said I had to apply here."

"Oh, that's awesome to hear. Congratulations." We both begin walking to the elevator together and he tells me about everything he did after graduating from high school. I just stand there and nod along, not knowing what else to do. We step into the elevator and I push for floor two.

"So do you want to maybe go get a coffee sometime or something?" he asks.

"I don't think that's such a great idea, I'm sorry." The elevator dings, signifying that we've reached the second floor and the doors open. I step out of the elevator saying goodbye. He stops the door and follows me.

"Listen, Samantha, I know things ended badly with us, but I really wish you could just let things go."

He isn't serious right now, is he? Things ended horribly; if only he knew. The only good thing that came from our relationship was Micah; which he knows nothing about. I ignore him and walk into the daycare. I grab Micah's bag and hold onto his hand while signing him out. As I walk back towards the elevator I can tell Louis expression has shifted.

"Samantha, I didn't know."

Of course he didn't because I never told him.

Apologies

Louis POV

I stood there like an idiot, wondering why she got off on this floor; I was still confused as to what floor this was until she walked out hand-in-hand with a little boy. I don't know what I was expecting, but it sure wasn't that. She walked to the elevator, and I tried to catch up, but she was gone. I couldn't believe she had a kid.

I walked to my car and drove back to my apartment. I quickly searched through a phone book, I thought I had no use for, and I look for the last name. I find the name, Samantha Foreman. I pulled my phone out and dialed the number. It rang and took me to voice mail, so I hung up and tried again; that's when a familiar voice answered.

"Hello?"

"Samantha, please just hear me out. I'm really sorry about earlier, I never meant what I said. I feel like an ass." It's quiet for a second and then I can tell her reaction changes.

"You are an ass." She laughs through the phone.

16

"So about that coffee, I actually really would like to go get some. Do you think maybe on Friday? I could give you some time to think about it if you want?"

"Friday is good for me, actually. Say 4:00 o'clock? I have the day off for my son's doctor appointment."

"Okay, that's great. I look forward to it. Bye, Samantha."

"Goodbye, Louis."

I didn't deserve this chance to reconnect with her after what happened, but I'm happy she was giving this to me. I ordered some pizza and rented a movie on TV, and I ended up falling asleep on the couch dreaming about a certain beautiful face.

Samantha's POV

The rest of the week flies by fast, I wake up at eight instead of my usual six o'clock. I get Micah dressed and take him upstairs to cook breakfast. My dad watches him while I go and take a shower. I pull on a pair of jeans and a gray Nike sweater and pull my hair up into a bun. My plan for the day is to take Micah to his appointment and then hang out at the park for a bit before I have to meet up with Louis. I check my watch and it's only 11 o'clock. I go back upstairs and watch TV with Micah while my dad goes to his office down the hall.

I decide to take a nap with Micah for a bit so I turn a Pandora radio station on and set my alarm for an hour. I didn't really sleep - I just laid there and thought about a lot of stuff while stroking Micah's little curls on the nape of his neck. My dad comes down and tells me he's going to get Sophie early from the airport so he won't be able to watch Micah later.

"I can just take him with me – it's fine, Dad."

"Are you sure, sweetie? I could just take him with me if you really need me to."

"It's okay, Dad, really. I'll see you guys when we get back then."

Micah wakes up after hearing us talk, I assume. He hugs my dad goodbye and goes to turn our TV on. My dad gives me a quick hug and a kiss on the forehead before he goes back upstairs to get ready to leave.

I check my watch and it's almost one o'clock. I leave Micah to watch TV for a bit longer while I go up to make him a sandwich before we get ready to leave. I'm kind of nervous to bring him along with me to go meet Louis for coffee. I know it's probably not the best thing to keep such a big secret from Louis, but I just don't know

18

how he'd react. I put some salad in a bowl for myself and bring Micah down his sandwich.

"Okay buddy, it's time to go see Dr. Mallow."

"He gives me stickers!"

I get Micah buckled into his car seat and we drive to his doctor's appointment. After all the testing on Micah, we schedule the next appointment and leave just before 3:30. I get Micah into his car seat and we drive to the coffee shop.

I get a small table in the back and order my usual coffee and an apple juice for Micah. That's when I see Louis walk in, and he looks around the coffee shop before he spots us.

You're such a whore, Sam, who does it in the bathroom at a fucking party?

Junior year broke me in more ways than I could count. I was the laughing stalk at school and I was known as the girl who slept with a guy in the bathroom at a party. All because of my stupid ex-boyfriend, Louis, who claimed he never said anything, but I know he did. He took me to this really fancy hotel and covered the place in rose petals. We dated for two years and he wanted to

19

make things "special" for our anniversary. But that was never in any of the rumors. All people figured was that I was another party girl who did it in the bathroom with her boyfriend. They didn't know anything.

I had loved Louis so much, and I had known he loved me. That's why I could never figure out why he'd start rumors like he did. He was so special, and secretly, I still think he kind of is.

Louis POV

There she is, beautiful as ever. I walk over and sit with her and Michael, or was it Micah? Their drinks come and I order mine. As I'm thinking of what to say, she speaks up.

"I know you're probably wondering who this is. Micah, this is my friend Louis, can you say 'hi'?"

"Hi," he says with a mouthful of cookie our waitress gave him.

"Louis, this is my son Micah."

"Hi, Micah, it's nice to meet you."

He continues eating his cookie and drinking his juice, holding onto Samantha's arm. I wonder if she has a boyfriend; his father perhaps. Micah can't be that old. I'm

lost in my thoughts, before I realize
Samantha is speaking to me.

"I'm really sorry, Louis," wait what?
"I've been mad at you for so long since high
school and I just feel like I really owe you
an apology. I know things ended, well,
horribly, but I would really like to start
over."

"You don't have to apologize for
anything, Samantha; I was the one who
wasn't there for you. After you left me I had
no clue what to do, but now I realize I
should have fought for you. All those stupid
rumors were so pathetic and cruel."

"Wait! You thought I broke up with
you? I never said that, one of your friends
told me that you were with another girl and
said to pass on the message. That night at
the party, I wasn't in there with anyone; I
was too busy getting sick at three in the
morning."

"I got a text from you saying things were
over, and then I heard all the rumors. People
were saying you hooked up with a guy in the
bathroom, and all these other horrible things.
I don't want to get worked up over this, but
it was all in the past, and I think we should
move on from it."

My drink is served and the waitress says
we have a really cute kid; I blush knowing

he's not mine, but for the sake of things right now I just smile and nod and Samantha goes along with it. I'd love it if he were mine, having kids with her was always a dream of mine when we were together. Of course it would have been later on in our relationship. I love Samantha so much.

"So to change the conversation, what's been up with you?" I ask.

"Well if you couldn't tell by now, I have a kid" she laughs. "Micah is three going to be turning four in just a few weeks. I dropped out shortly after I found out I was pregnant with him, but I got my diploma online a few years ago."

"I always wondered why you left; I thought it was because, you know, the rumors and stuff. I would have never guessed that you were pregnant."

"I started working at Morises shortly after he was born. Sophie got me the job, and I was lucky enough to get the paid internship and free daycare."

I wonder again, where's his dad? She hasn't mentioned a guy in the picture.

"So enough about me, what have you been up to, Mr. College graduate?" She takes a sip from her coffee and looks at me with those beautiful brown eyes.

"Not much since I graduated, I took a few months off after high school, then I had the interest to want to go to college. I majored in English and literature, two classes I hated most in high school. Go figure right? Anyways, I did that and ended up here, I never thought I'd get the manager position."

"Sophie told me about you. She said you had the best interview. You were a bit nervous, but she said you passed with flying colors. I asked her about you the other day."

I spit out some of the coffee I had just sipped after what she just told me. How the heck does she know my boss, well technically, *our* boss? After cleaning my mouth and the stain off my pants, I see that she's laughing at me. Laughing!

"How do you know Sophie?"

"She's our boss, and she happens to be married to my father. Did I not mention that part? I know you two only met a few times when we dated, but I thought you would've remembered her." She laughs.

We talked for hours it felt like, when I check the time I realize we've been here for almost over an hour. Talking to her like this was always so amazing; when we dated it was like this all the time. It was never brought up or mentioned, but I wonder who his father is? Lost in my thoughts I realize I'm starring at Micah.

Samantha's POV

I haven't talked with anybody for this long in forever it seems like; Louis and I were always like this, though, when we were together. He talked mostly about what he did in college, but I could tell he was wondering what most people wonder. Who and where is Micah's dad?

"Curious, right?" I ask.

"I mean, well yeah. I don't mean to sound rude and I apologize for staring, but yeah, I was a little curious." He tells me nervously. I look to Micah as he's playing a game on my phone, getting bored of our conversation.

"Most people are. I don't mind at all but I prefer not to talk about it really. Anyways it's getting kind of late so I think we should probably go. Thanks for paying for the coffee," I grab my jacket and Micah's bag and we head to the door to leave. "So I'll see you at work tomorrow, boss." I jokingly say, while getting Micah into his car seat.

"Sounds good, I'll see you tomorrow. Goodnight Micah. Night Samantha." He waves goodbye to Micah in the backseat and

I give him a hug before getting into the car myself.

If you ask me, the date went pretty well, even though it was just coffee. I drive home and run a quick bath for Micah before getting him to bed. As I'm walking out of the bathroom after changing for bed I get a text on my phone, from Louis.

"I had a great day; thanks for letting me meet your little man. Night, xo."

First Dates

Samantha's POV

So it's been a few weeks now since Louis and I went out for coffee. I've been swamped with work and also planning Micah's birthday party this coming weekend. I check my watch as I'm heading out the door from work, I might have time to run to the store before I have to meet Louis for dinner tonight. Of all things he sends me an email, asking if I would go out to dinner with him tonight, and he wants Micah to tag along, as well. It's four o'clock right now and our dinner is scheduled for seven, but I still have to go home and change.

I stop on the second floor as always, and sign Micah out of daycare. I get him settled in his car seat and we drive to Party City. He's been really enjoying that new kid show on TV, *Jake and the Neverland Pirates*, so we begin walking down the party decorations aisle searching for the pirate theme. Micah points it out to me and there is a really nice selection. I decide on some fun party games some plates, balloons and other party necessities. We go to check out and

Micah points out the big balloon, in the shape of the number four on the wall, so I decide to have them add that to the bill.

Once we get home, it's just after five o'clock. I bring everything down to my room and set it all on my bed before I start to pick out my outfit for the night. I change Micah into a pair of jeans and a cute plaid button up shirt before he goes upstairs to see my Dad and Sophie to watch TV while I get ready.

I blow dry my hair after getting out of the shower and decide to put it up into a nice bun rather than taking the extra time to curl it. I put light makeup on, and change into the black fitted dress I got a few years ago from Sophie for my birthday. It's not too fancy, just solid black with lace on the sleeves and a small cut out on the back. I check myself in the mirror once more before slipping on my black flats. I grab my phone and Micah's bag before going up to get him.

I check my phone and see a text from Louis.

Can't wait to see you two tonight! xo

I check the time and its 6:45; Louis should be here any minute. He's usually always early. Just as I predicted, Louis is at the door at 6:50. Micah and I wave bye to my Dad and Sophie, and my dad comes to the door to shake Louis's hand before seeing us out. I stop at my car and begin to grab Micah's car seat to put in Louis car before Louis suggests we just take my car instead of hauling Micah's car seat back and forth.

"So where is this secret place you're taking us tonight?" I ask.

"That's for me to know and you to find out."

"This is really sweet of you, you know?"

"Sweet is what I do best, Samantha."

After about ten minutes Louis finally exits the freeway. Once I see the sign, I know where he's taking us. He knows it's my favorite restaurant and a pretty kid friendly place - he knows us so well. We pull into the parking lot and he gets out of the car and runs to our side and opens my door for me. He helps Micah get out of his car seat and takes his hand to walk, Micah reaches out for my hand and I take hold of it while we walk in.

We don't have to wait long for a table because Louis reserved one the other day, knowing it was probably going to be pretty busy tonight for the big college football game. We take our seats and get a booster seat for Micah. Our waiter comes over and asks us for our drink orders, I order Micah an Apple juice and strawberry lemonade for myself and Louis gets just a coke.

"So how did Micah's doctor's appointment go the other day, you sounded kind of worried."

"His hearing is getting worse, they said, they put him on some new medication but it won't slow it down much longer. They think I should get him into some signing classes soon, and that I should start learning to sign, too. It's all just happening really fast and I don't know what to do."

Micah was born slightly deaf. The doctors told me that his hearing would only get worse as he got older. Now that he's almost four, they tell me his hearing will be gone within the next year. It's taken a huge toll on my life what with all the doctors' appointments and hearing aids, and the class we take every Sunday with other kids his age to learn to sign. I'm not even worried about him learning to sign, or even all the medical bills, I'm just worried about how he'll be treated once he's older. And the fact that this is all happening so fast.

Kisses

Louis POV

As I'm in Toys R Us looking for a gift for Micah I think back to when I used to work here in high school. I remember when Sam would stop by and bring-

"Louis?" I hear someone say from behind me.

I turn to see my old manager, Mackenzie. She's organizing some things on a shelf behind me. She must work here still.

"What are you looking for?"

"I'm trying to look for something for a four year olds birthday, I thought the toys were in this aisle but I guess not." I laugh

"Aisle three, are you looking for anything specific?"

"Jake and the Neverland Pirates, at least I think that's what she told me."

"Ah, yeah that would be down aisle four. You should find all the pirate stuff down there." She walks me to the aisle which is filled with all types of pirate themed toys.

"Jake and the Neverland Pirates," she says, pointing to the multiple themed toys

"Thanks, I guess things have changed in the five years I was gone."

"Yeah, I heard you took off for college. How did that work out for you?" She asks.

"I got hired recently over at Morises. They hired me as manager in one of the departments."

"Oh that's great; yeah I've been stuck here since graduation. The pay is good, but who wants to be stuck here, right? So who is the gift for, you got a kid?"

"Not mine. A friend of mine has a son and his birthday is tomorrow."

"Oh cool, well it was nice seeing you. Maybe I'll see you around."

I pick out a few different toys and go to check out; I decide to pay extra for them to wrap them for me. I can't believe how fast this kid has bonded with me. I get everything into a party bag and set it in the back seat. I get back home and have a few voicemails on my machine. I hit play and listen as I get something to drink in the fridge.

"Hey Louis, I was wondering if you could come over later and help me set up. My dad went out with Sophie tonight and they are stuck in traffic and won't be here until late this evening. Kyle went out with his friends tonight so he isn't able to help. Micah is in bed right now and I want to surprise him with breakfast in the morning. His party is in the afternoon so I don't know if I'll have time to set up in between. I'm sorry for intruding, and it's okay if you can't-" Beep.

I grab my phone out of my pocket and see that it's dead. I put it on the charger and call her from the house phone.

"Hey, I can be over in like ten minutes to help."

"Thanks so much, Louis. I'm ordering pizza, so I can pay you with that."

"You know the way to my heart. I'll see you soon."

I grab my charger and change really quick before heading to her house. I pull into her driveway just as the pizza delivery guy is leaving. I knock and walk in after she yells for me to come in. She's in the kitchen grabbing some plates and cups for us. I go to help her and end up slipping on something wet on the floor and bring her down with me.

"Louis, oh my god, I'm so sorry. Are you okay?"

"I'm fine, are you okay?"

"I must have spilt something earlier while looking for my keys."

"It's fine." I laugh, helping her to her feet. "Why were you looking for your keys?"

"I have to go to the bakery in town and pick up Micah's cake before eight and I totally forgot until I called you a little while ago."

I check the clock and its 6:30. Ok we have about an hour.

"I could run and get it, I have my car."

"You don't have to, Louis."

"I want to, it's fine. How about you call and let them know I'm coming to pick it up. Is it paid for?"

"Yeah, it's on my card. Thank you so much, Louis."

I pick up the cake from the bakery, and get it in the back of my car. I drive back to Samantha's house and carry the cake and my gifts I bought earlier in. I set the cake and the gifts on the counter that she cleared while I was gone. I go to the living room where she's setting things up.

"I put the cake on the counter."

"You're a life saver, Louis, thank you so much. My dad called and they are an hour away - still in traffic. It's crazy."

"Well, I'm here to help. What do you need me to do?"

"Well, the party is going to be in here, so maybe help move around the furniture and put it in the den down the hall. For more space to let the kids play, and then also over in the dining area, I want to tie some of the balloons on the chairs."

I grab Sam's shoulders and pull her into a hug. I can tell she's stressing out.

"Everything is going to be perfect for his birthday tomorrow. Don't worry." I run my fingers through her hair and give her a kiss on her forehead and we begin moving the furniture to the den.

After about an hour of moving stuff and putting up decorations her mom and dad finally get home. He apologizes for not being able to help but she assures him its fine and that I was here to help her. Her mom offers to help cook breakfast in the morning and her dad tells Sam that the bouncy house he rented should be here tomorrow morning, just before the party.

Samantha's POV

"Dad, you really didn't have to, it's fine."

"Sweetheart, I insist. My grandson only turns four once in his life. Please let me do this for him."

I finally agree and he and Sophie go off to bed for the night. Louis helps me tie the rest of the balloons to the chairs and I tell him I'm sorry for intruding on his night.

"Sam you're not intruding at all, I thought this was a pretty fun night. Micah is a cool kid, and I think he has a pretty awesome mom."

"Thanks for helping - it really means a lot. I'm just ready for tomorrow already, I hope he loves everything."

"He's going to love it, I promise you. Everything is going to be great tomorrow."

I check the time on my phone, and it's almost nine o'clock. We spent almost two hours decorating and I realized we didn't even touch the pizza.

"Oh my god, I bet your starving. I totally forgot about eating."

"Cold pizza it is then. That sounds good to me." He laughs.

Louis POV

"Louis, could I ask you something?"

"Anything," I can tell she thinks about it for a second before she finally asks.

"Do you think we could have made things different?"

I think about what I'm going to say for a minute before I finally speak. "Sam, what happened in high school was us being teenagers. We let something come between our relationship, and I should have stood up for you. But I still love you, Sam, and I think I always will."

Our bodies have shifted and are somehow closer now, as if the universe is trying to draw us back to each other. I place

35

my hand on her soft, now rosy red cheeks, and kiss her. It wasn't just any kiss, it was our kiss. I entwine my other hand with hers and tell her she should probably go to bed. She says I can sleep down on the couch tonight if I want to. I take up her offer to sleep on the couch and she finds me some shorts to wear to bed.

"Sam," she turns her head at the perfect angle and I see her gorgeous face through the dim lighting.

"Yeah,"

"Goodnight."

"Goodnight."

More Than This

Samantha's POV

I wake up the next morning to my alarm clock and I roll myself out of bed a few minutes later. I do my usual morning routine and go to wake up Micah and give him a bath, but he's not in his bed. I start to think that maybe he went upstairs already and saw his surprise. Luckily, he didn't. He and Louis are sitting on the couch watching Cars on the TV, still in their pajamas. I go and sit next to them and tell Micah, "Happy Birthday", kissing him on his cheek.

"Mama, I'm four." He tells me.

"Wow, you're getting so big. You need to stop growing, you little munchkin."

I tickle his tummy and watch the movie with them for a few minutes before I tell Louis I'm going to go get ready. I lay out a floral print sundress that Micah picked out for me last week; I grab my towel and do my business in the shower. After quickly getting dressed, and blow drying my hair I go to get Micah and put him in the bath. He picks out the new outfit grandpa got him - a shirt with Jake and the other pirates on it and his matching jeans and boots. I put his new hearing aids on him, the ones the doctor wants him to start adjusting to. He sits and watches the rest of the movie while Louis goes to take a shower.

"Mama, is Louis your boyfriend?"

"No honey, he's just mommy's friend."

"I think he loves you, Mama."

Just as I'm about to respond, Louis walks out in the same clothes he wore yesterday, and he's trying his best to dry his damp hair with the towel. Why is he always so damn sexy? Louis offers to watch Micah while I go up and see if Sophie needs any help with breakfast.

"Morning, where's the little birthday boy?" Sophie asks as I walk into the kitchen.

"Louis stayed over and he's down there watching him. Do you need help with anything?" She passes me a mixing spoon and has me stir Micah's favorite pancake mix.

"An overnighter?" she asks, giving me a devious smile.

"It's not like that, he slept on the couch."

"It was really nice of him to come and help you set up last night. Your dad and I are really sorry we couldn't help."

"Yeah, we had a good time." I don't notice the smile on my face until I realize Sophie is smiling, as well.

"We've noticed you've been having some good times together lately."

I just shake my head and continue to stir the pancake mix before getting ready to place it on the hot pan in front of me. After sprinkling the last chocolate chip pancake with sprinkles and frying the last pieces of bacon we're finally almost done. I set the table as Sophie puts everything on serving plates. I walk down to the basement and get Micah and Louis.

"Close your eyes, Micah," I say while walking him up the stairs.

"Do I have a surprise, mama?"

"Open your eyes and see!"

He uncovers his eyes and looks around the room for a second before turning around to me with a huge smile on his face.

"Mama, is all this for me?"

"It's for your birthday, do you like it, buddy?"

He runs to me and gives me a hug, and almost brings me to tears when he signs to me he loves me. I sign back to him and tell him I love him too. I whisper in his ear that Louis also helped me with everything and he hugs him and tells him thank you.

"Anything for my favorite little guy. Happy birthday, buddy. I'll see you later, okay? I'll be back for your party."

"Okay. Bye, Louis." Micah runs over and gives my dad and Sophie a hug, and she helps him get settled in a chair at the table.

I walk to the front door with Louis and I wonder if I should ask why he's leaving, but I don't want to sound like a desperate girlfriend, who always needs him around. I'm not his girlfriend, he's just my friend.

"Is my cooking not well enough for you or something?" I playfully ask.

"No it's not that, I have a meeting today with someone and it's really important. But it's only about an hour, so I'll be able to make his party."

"I'm not your girlfriend, Louis; you don't have to tell me where you're going all the time."

"Well, I wish you were." The words come out of his mouth before even he knows it, I think.

"I can't, I already told you."

I walk Louis out to his car which is just parked next to mine. I wish he would stop bringing up us dating; we talked about this last week.

"That's not what you were saying last week, Samantha. You know you want to kiss me again."

He's right, I do want to kiss him again, but I'm not going to admit that to him. He dropped me off after we had dinner last week and it was just a little moment we had. I don't think it meant anything - to him at least.

"So what if I do," and before I even finish my sentence his lips are against mine.

"I knew you wanted to," he says as our foreheads come together.

"I'll see you when you get back," I say, stepping a few feet back as he gets into his car.

"Yes, you will, and by the way you look beautiful." He shuts his car door and starts his engine and waves goodbye.

Birthday Party

Samantha's POV

I bring Micah back downstairs and put the TV on for him while Sophie, my Dad, and I clear away breakfast and start putting together the goody bags. I check the time and we have about an hour until Micah's friends will be here, and the guys setting up the bouncy house should be here any minute.

"So how are things with you and Louis, sweetheart?" My dad asks.

"Things are good. He was so nice to come and help me last night. We ended up staying up after and talking for a while."

"We noticed. But, sweetheart, you know you're going to have to tell him. I mean sooner or later-"

"Dad, I know I need to tell him it's just..." I finish wrapping the last bag when the doorbell rings and our conversation is cut short.

"Your dad just wants what's best for you and Micah. I think you should consider talking about it with him soon, I think he deserves to know the truth." Sophie gives me a hug and kisses my forehead.

I know nobody can replace my mother, but Sophie makes a really amazing step mom. I know she'll always be here for me, and I really love her for treating me like her daughter. I set all the goody bags in the basket near the front door so I don't forget to pass them out as people leave.

I call the pizza guys and order ten pizzas for the party, Micah comes up after the bouncy house is finished being set up. His eyes nearly pop out of his head with excitement. Everyone shows up a few minutes later and our backyard is swamped with kids. Mostly the kids here are from the daycare at work and a few are from Micah's new signing class.

"What a party," a familiar voice says from behind me.

"Zach, I can't believe you made it!" I turn around and give him a hug.

Zach and I met when I was doing online school, he lives a few blocks down from us and he used to tutor me. He really liked me, but nothing ever happened between us - besides a few make out sessions once or twice.

"I wouldn't miss my little buddy's fourth birthday party." He sets his gift down with the rest of them and Micah comes running over and gives him a hug.

I know some people look at Zach and think he's a badass kind of guy but he's totally not. He has a lot of tattoos and dresses differently but he's the sweetest guy I know, plus he's super smart. We sit at the table inside and he talks about his recent trip to London.

"So your brother told me you've been seeing someone," he says out of the blue.

"You still talk to my brother?"

"Don't dodge the question Sam. Who's the guy?"

"Nobody you need to worry about. Him and I, we're just friends."

"'Just friends' who happened to have kissed earlier?"

"Dammit, Kyle, is such a creep. And just for the record, Louis kissed me." Shit.

"Louis? Your Louis? The jerk that broke your heart back at your old school?"

"Yeah; but Zach-"

He grabs me by the arm and brings me down to the basement. I wish I hadn't told him everything.

"Sam, you have to be fucking kidding me. Louis?"

"Zach, he's not the same guy he was when I was dating him. And I may have made things look worse than what they actually were."

"Does he know? About, Micah?"

"Hell no! Zach could you please just calm down for a second."

"Everything you told me about him, made him look like a piece of shit. He hurt you and then left you, Sam."

"He didn't leave me."

"What?"

"He didn't leave me, things got mixed up and everything was just complicated. He loved me, Zach. He told me himself."

"And you're going to believe that garbage?"

"Could you please calm down? I don't want to make a scene at my son's birthday party."

Louis POV

"... I don't want to make a scene at my son's birthday party, now you can either calm down or leave Zach." I hear Sam's voice downstairs and I wonder who she's talking to.

A few minutes later a guy with tattoos lining up his arms and black skinny jeans comes walking up from the basement. He walks straight out the door and gets into his car, speeding out of the neighborhood. I start walking down the stairs when I hear soft crying from the bathroom. What the hell happened?

"Samantha?"

"Just go away," I hear her voice from the bathroom.

I open the door, and she's sitting in the bathtub with her knees at her chest and tears coming down her face. What the hell happened while I was gone?

"Samantha, are you okay?"

"Leave me alone, just go away, Louis."

I put down the toilet seat and sit down. I grab the tissue box sitting on the counter and pass a few to her. She takes them and wipes her eyes and nose. Even when she's crying, I still see the beauty in her. She stands up out of the tub and, to my surprise, wraps her arms around me and sits on my lap. I run my hand through her hair, and she lays her head on my shoulder.

"I love you," she whispers in my ear.

"I love you." I kiss her shoulder and she gets up.

She looks at herself in the mirror and fixes her hair. She takes some more tissue and wipes off some of the mascara that ran down her face.

"I really want to kiss you again," she blushes looking down at her feet and playing with my hand in hers.

I stand up and put my hand on her soft cheek. I kiss her gently at first and then I wrap both of my arms around her waist and hold her up against the bathroom wall. This is what I've missed the most. I know this isn't just any kiss - it's one filled with love and passion one that can be shared with only one person. And that's Samantha. After catching our breath I grab her hand and we walk upstairs together.

Samantha's POV

It's been half an hour since Louis and I were downstairs. He helps me get all the kids together for some games before we start eating and opening presents. After a few rounds of musical chairs and pin the tail on the donkey we get everyone inside at the table to eat pizza. I get Micah into his big birthday chair and I bring everyone the pizza to choose from. I serve Micah a piece of pepperoni with pineapple, our favorite, and Sophie grabs the juice boxes from the fridge for everyone.

"Sam, can we talk?" I feel a hand on my shoulder and I turn to see Zach standing behind me.

I follow him outside to the patio.

"I'm sorry for acting the way I did. It was so unlike me. I was just trying to look out for you; I don't want to see you get hurt by that jackass."

"I forgive you, Zach, and I know some things might have happened between us a long time ago but it can't happen anymore."

"There will always be a special place in my heart for you, Sam," he gives me a hug and we go back inside.

"Present time!" My dad hollers to everyone.

Kyle and he go out and get all the gifts people brought that were out on the back porch. I help them set everything in front of Micah on the floor in the living room and I sit with Micah to help him open them. The first one he grabs is from my Dad and Sophie. I pull out the card and read it to Micah.

"To our favorite little guy, we wish you the best birthday ever! We love you so much. Love, Nam and Papa." Micah pulls the tissue paper out of the bag and pulls out a brand new Nabi kids tablet with a Jake and the Neverland Pirates game.

"Thank you Papa and Nam Nam." He stands up to give my Dad and Sophie a hug.

He gets a few other toys from some of his friends and then he opens Louis's present next. There is a card on top, so I pull it out and read it to him.

"Micah, Happy fourth Birthday, little man. I'm glad I could share this special day with you and your mom. You're such a cool little dude and I'm glad I got to know you. Have a great day, buddy!"

There are three different things wrapped up in the bag, so he pulls them out one by one and opens them. The first one is a toy set of his favorite TV show. The second one is a toy truck. The third one is a plastic toy box with, yet again, his favorite TV show characters, in Lego pieces.

Micah quickly gets up, and wraps his arms around Louis. Politely thanking him for the presents before returning back to the floor, to open the rest of his gifts.

After opening the last few presents, and thanking everyone, we finally get ready to sing happy birthday. My dad grabs the cake and sets it in front of Micah, at the table. He lights the candles and we all start singing.

Happy Birthday, Micah!

Almost

Samantha's POV

I didn't tell you this morning, but you look very beautiful today. XO
From, Louis T
3:47 pm
Awe, thanks. I want to do something tonight, just you and I. We need to talk.
From, Samantha F
3:55 pm
How does Carrino's sound, say around eight? I have an important meeting today after work.
From, Louis T
4:00 pm
I'll meet you there. Have a fun meeting!
From, Samantha F
4:15 pm
I grab my purse and some manuscripts to finish tonight. I log off my computer and walk to the elevator, when my cell phone rings. I push for floor two and dig around in my purse before finding my phone; and Zach's name lights up on the screen.

"Hey, what's up?"

"Nothing, are you off?" he asks.

"Yeah, just going to get Micah and then I'm heading home. Why?"

"Let me come get you guys, we can go get some frozen yogurt."

"You'd have to get here in, like, super speed." I sign Micah out and take his hand in mine.

"Already here!"

When we get off the elevator, sure enough, Zach is standing by the entrance to the building. He's wearing his usual leather jacket and ripped skinny jeans. He puts out his cigarette before we get outside.

"Zach!" Micah shouts while running into his arms.

"Hey little man, what's up."

"Nothing," he answers politely.

"You want to go get some ice cream?!"

"Yes! Mommy, can we?"

"Of course, buddy." I decide that Micah and I will just follow Zach to the frozen yogurt place in town instead of him driving us.

I check the time and it's already 4:30. We go inside and I let Micah pick out everything to go on our shared frozen yogurt. He piles on M&Ms and a bunch of crushed Oreo just the way we both like it. Zach kindly pays for ours and we all take a seat.

"So how's work going?"

"Work is good. I've just been really busy lately."

"Oh, yeah, I bet. So you and him are like a thing now?"

"Zach, we talked about this-"

"*You* talked about it. All I'm saying is, I think the guy is a d-i-c-k," he spells the last part not wanting to say the word around Micah.

"We're not dating. Louis and I are simply friends."

"Your brother tells me otherwise."

"My brother doesn't know anything, he just thinks he does."

"Sam, I know you might have stopped caring about me after we broke up, but I still have feelings for you and I don't like the idea of seeing you around with someone like him." He isn't serious, right? I love Zach, as a friend, of course, but when he starts acting like this, it really upsets me.

"You can't just tell me that in front of my son, Zach. And for the record, we never dated and I've never stopped caring about you. I think we should go. I'll talk to you when you start acting like a real friend."

I tell Micah we're leaving and he hugs Zach goodbye.

When we get home I decide to take a quick shower while my dad watches Micah for me. I put on a pair of my black leggings

52

and a pink top with a gray cardigan, I check my phone on the charger and I don't have any texts from Louis. I go and join Micah on the couch and we watch his TV show for an hour before it's his bedtime.

I tuck him into his bed and put the Lion King on his small TV. I lay with him for a little while until he falls asleep, I kiss his forehead before getting up to turn off his TV. I check my phone again. I have a text from Louis and a missed phone call from Zach.

I text Louis back, telling him I'll be outside in five minutes to meet him. I decide on a pair of shoes while I hold my phone to my ear with my shoulder while I call Zach back. It goes to voicemail so I hang up and decide to just try again later.

"Hey beautiful," Louis greets me with a kiss on the cheek as I buckle my seat belt.

I try my best to fake a smile but I can't stop thinking about what happened earlier today with Zach. The drive to Carrino's is short and I feel bad for feeling like this on our date. This isn't a date. My stupid subconscious reminds me as we get out of the car. I let Louis entwine his hand with mine as the hostess takes us to our seats and places a menu in front of us.

"Can I get you guys started with something to drink?" She asks politely pulling out her pen and paper from her apron.

"I'll have a sprite and lemon water please." I tell her.

"I'll have the same," he tells her.

She leaves us with a smile and tells us our server will be here shortly to take our orders. I scan the menu when I see Louis shuffling in his seat.

"So how's Micah?"

"He's fine; he was asleep when you picked me up. Actually there's something about that-"

"Mrs. Foreman," I turn to the older man standing next to our table who was asking for my attention.

"I'm sorry to interrupt, but you have a phone call here."

"Oh, okay." I set my menu down and excuse myself from the table while I follow the man to the front of the restaurant. He hands me a phone that's connected to the wall, I take a second before picking it up.

"Hello?"

I hear breathing on the other end, and before I start thinking I'm just imagining things, the voice on the other end speaks up.

"Samantha, hi I - I need you to come get me."

"Zach?"

"I tried texting but you didn't answer, your brother said you were at Carrino's with that stupid piece of sh-"

"Stop it Zach, I left my phone on silent I'm sorry. Where are you?"

"Old highway 99, I'm here at Jimmy's bar and I drank a lot and I forgot my wallet. They are so stupid here and said I have to pay."

"Dammit. Of course you have to pay it's a bar for god sake! I'll be there in 20 minutes, don't go anywhere."

I hang up the phone in frustration and walk back to the table.

"What's wrong?"

"I'm sorry but could you drive me back to my house?"

"Yeah, of course. Is everything okay?"

"Yeah, it's just my friend is stuck at a bar and he's drunk, so he needs me to come get him."

"I can just drive, it's no big deal." I accept Louis offer for him to drive and he pays for our drinks and we leave.

The drive is long because the bar Zach is at is just right outside of town. I check the time on my phone and it's only 8:45, what the hell was he thinking getting drunk this early?

"I'm really sorry about all this, I ruined our date." I look at Louis and he just laughs.

"What?" I ask him. He takes my hand in his and brings it to his lips and kisses it softly, making me blush.

"I didn't know we were considering that a date. So does that mean we're dating than?"

I think about his question for a second before nodding my head in response.

"Yeah, I guess so." I say in almost a whisper.

He smiles and entwines his fingers with mine. It takes us 15 minutes to get through traffic on the freeway until we finally come to the exit where Zach is. Louis parks the car in the front of the bar; I unbuckle my seat belt and get out of the car. Before closing my door I tell Louis to wait in the car.

"I'll be right here when you come out."

I go inside and look around before I see a drunken Zach sitting by the bar, I can already tell this isn't going to be fun. I walk over and it takes him a second before he notices me.

"Samantha!" He says with excitement.

I look at the bartender who is obviously pissed and annoyed at this point. I pull out my wallet and give him a twenty and let him keep the change. I pull his arm around my shoulder and walk him out of the bar.

"You're so pretty, you know, I love it."

Before getting him to the car he hurls over and spills his drunken stomach in a bush nearby. Louis gets out of the car to help and that's when things turn upside down.

"Who the hell is this asshole and what is he doing here!" Zach says walking towards Louis. Before he gets any closer I step in between him and Louis.

"Zach, he's my friend and he drove me here to come and save your ass."

"I don't need your stupid help, Samantha."

"Oh really, because I just paid your fucking bar tab after your drunken ass got wasted. We were having a nice evening and you had to ruin it-" before I can finish my sentence Louis grabs my arm and pulls me away from Zach.

"Everyone, just calm down. Now mate, I think you should get in the car so we can leave."

Zach climbs into the back seat, and as I try to contain myself from crying, Louis pulls me into a hug. I fit my head into his shoulder and let a few tears fall.

"You're a good friend you know?" He whispers in my ear.

"I'm sorry for freaking out like that. That was so unlike me, he just pissed me off."

"You don't have to apologize to me Sam, I understand. We should probably get him to his house, don't you think?"

"Yeah, he lives just down the street from me so you can just drive us to my house."

We get back into the car and Louis drives us back to my place. I help Zach out of the car and he sits on the sidewalk while I get my purse out of Louis car. I apologize again for ruining the night, and we plan to reschedule our dinner another time, before leaving Louis reaches for my hand and pulls me in for a kiss. I wish him a goodnight and promise to text him later, and then he's off. I grab Zach and pull his arm around my shoulder and we start walking to his house.

"He doesn't love you like I do, Sam," he says while staggering on the sidewalk.

"You don't know what you're talking about Zach, you're drunk."

"I could give you more than him, because I really love you."

"Could we just drop this, please, my night has been shitty enough as it is. I don't want to argue with you while you're drunk."

"I'm not drunk Sam, I just had a few beers." He stops in his tracks and wraps his other arm around me.

"Zach, stop it!"

"You're so beautiful Sam; I just wish he didn't take you from me."

"Nobody took me away from you, we were never together Zach. You're my friend, and that's that." We finally arrive to Zach's house and I dig around in my purse for the spare key he gave me.

"Will you come in, please?"

"No Zach, I need to go home. I'll call you tomorrow. Let's get you to the couch."

After getting him situated on the couch, in his living room, I pull his shoes off while he drifts off to sleep. I grab a blanket from the closet and put it over his sleeping body.

I know Zach means well, but when he drinks it's like he's a totally different person, and I hate it. Even though we did mess around a bit, it never went further than that. I thought he understood that, but apparently not. I slip out the door and lock it behind me. I check the time on my phone and it's after ten.

I drag myself down to my room after pouring myself a glass of water, and I start to hear crying. My pace changes as I rush into Micah's room, I switch his light on and see him sitting there cupping his hands over his ears and crying. No, no, no, not again. I rush to his side and hold him in my arms, I try to rock him back and forth, but I know anything I do won't stop this pain he's having.

"Shh, baby it's going to be okay. Mommy's here," I try holding back my tears because I know I need to be strong for him.

This only just started about a month ago and it's something that is a side effect of him losing his hearing so early on. I can't do anything about it but just hold him; the doctors say it needs to just happen. Whatever that means.

I hear footsteps and my dad walks into the room with his robe wrapped around him, his usual bed attire. He kneels down next to the bed and rubs my back while I rock Micah back and forth.

"It's going to be okay, sweetheart, you know that the doctors can't do anything to prevent this. Just holding him will help him." I nod my head and let a tear escape from my eyes.

After another ten minutes of holding him he finally takes his hands away from his ears. I hold him to my chest and let him fall back to sleep in my arms, I lay my head back on his headboard and let sleep take over me.

Office Time

Louis POV

It's been about a month now since Sam and I went on that - "half date" I'm going to call it. We didn't get to finish it because of that jerk friend of hers. We have talked almost every night, on the phone, since then and she suggested that we slow things down a bit in our relationship, if you could call it that. She wants to focus on Micah and his health. His hearing is getting worse, I guess. I'm not saying I'm upset about it, but I'm not happy about it, either. I love Samantha, and I just want to build our relationship and I definitely don't want to lose her again. But I know that with a kid, having a relationship can be pretty hard. If we had a child together I think things would be different between us - we would be so much closer, and I'd love her and our child unconditionally.

But that can't happen now - she already has a child and it's someone else's. That's another thing we never talked about - where was Micah's dad? Every time I bring it up she just tells me she doesn't want to talk about it. Is he dead? I wonder if maybe he just doesn't know; I don't see her holding news like that to herself, though.

"Mr. Melville?" I'm pulled from my thoughts as a young brunette walks into my office, grabbing my attention.

"Yeah, that's me. And you are?" She takes the seat in front of my desk and quickly gets up to shake my hand.

"My name is Leah. Leah Michelson, I'm here for an interview." She straightens her skirt out before sitting down again.

I quickly look at my computer and then down at my calendar, spread across my desk, and sure enough it's scribbled down that she has an interview with me today. Leah, interview at 1:30.

"Of course, sorry about that; I have been so busy - I totally forgot." Truth be told, I actually haven't been busy, I've been thinking about Samantha too much. This is my third interview now since I've worked here and I actually really enjoy them.

"That's fine, sir." She pulls out a red folder from her bag and grabs a few papers and hands them to me." Here is my résumé and I also have a letter of recommendation. It's just on the bottom there."

I scan over the papers and see that she just graduated from the same college I went to. Her degree is lower than my own and her letter is from my old English professor.

"I figured Mr. Davis would have retired by now," I laugh. The straight line across her face curves into a smile.

"You know Mr. Davis?"

"Yeah, I graduated a couple months ago from there." This is a pretty good resume and I know that if Mr. Davis wrote her a recommendation letter she must know what she's doing.

"He is my favorite professor there. He was actually the one who encouraged me to apply here for an internship."

I look over her papers again a few more times and ask her some mandatory interview questions.

"You're hired!" I tell her.

"Just like that?" she asks.

"There is some paperwork that Mandy will give you before you leave. She's just right outside my office. I'll walk you out." She grabs her purse from the floor and straightens out her blouse before following me.

I pass her onto Mandy who gathers the paperwork for her to fill out. I let her know she'll need to turn it in by Tuesday of next week. She nods her head and walks to the elevator and leaves after saying thank you again. I stroll over to a familiar desk and decide to pop in on a certain someone.

"Samantha, could I talk to you in my office for a second?" I say peeking behind her cubicle. She smiles up at me and sets her pen down before following me back to my office.

"What's up?" She asks plopping down in the chair.

"I just wanted to talk - see what's up."

"During office hours, Mr. Melville?" she giggles.

"I was thinking we could go for some coffee after work - you know to talk and stuff." I sound like an idiot.

"It'll have to be quick. Micah is home sick with my dad."

"Is everything okay, you know, with his hearing and stuff?" I can tell by the change of expression on her face that the answer is no, everything is not okay. My thoughts are answered when she shakes her head and looks down at her feet.

"What happened?" I ask further. I get up from my comfy chair behind my desk and move to the chair next to where she is sitting, I grab hold of her hand and take it in mine.

"He had one of his episodes again the other night - the ringing in his ears and stuff. I just couldn't bear sitting there with him while he was in so much pain. I felt helpless." I can tell she is trying her best not to cry right now. She keeps telling me she isn't going to cry because she needs to stay strong for him.

"I'm so sorry. He shouldn't be going through this. I wish there was a way I could help." I wrap my free arm around her and pull her into my chest. I kiss the top of her forehead before she tells me she should probably get back to work. I nod and give her one last hug. Before she goes, we plan to meet here in my office after everyone leaves later on.

Uh Oh!

Samantha's POV

After finishing my manuscripts for the day, I decide to check Facebook to pass some time before the day is over. I unlock my cell phone and smile a bit at the picture of Micah I have saved as my wallpaper - he's lying on my bed and his hair is a bit messy; he has the cutest smile on his face that just makes my heart melt. I don't know if I'm the only one who notices but Louis and Micah have the same smile. *Probably because that's his son* - my stupid subconscious reminds me.

I open the Facebook app and notice that I have an unread message; it must be from one of my cousins or something because I don't have many friends on here. I open the message icon and sure enough it's from my cousin, Shawn. He lives over in England right now and he's just a few years older than me. He was on my mom's side, so I didn't really see him much, because my aunt moved to England, and got married when I was really little. After my mom died they stopped coming for holiday visits.

Shawn: *Hey, I'm not sure if you remember me or not. I just wanted to let you know I'm moving over that way in a few months, I was wondering if you'd like to maybe get together and hang out sometime? Let me know.*

Samantha: *Hey Shawn! Of course I remember you. It's been a long time, hasn't it? Why are you moving over here, exactly?*

I wait for his response, and in the meantime check out his profile. I look at a few of his posts and then at some of his pictures. He aged well. I don't remember much about him - seeing as I was only two years old when I last saw him, but I remember how nice he was.

Shawn: *Too long, I heard you had a baby? Is that true? Sorry for all the questions. The reason I'm moving there is because I was offered a job. My old college professor told me good things about what they offer there, so he made some phone calls and this place offered me the job just like that.*

Samantha: *Wow, that's amazing! What kind of job, and where? I might know the place. To answer your question- yes, I did have a baby. He's not a baby anymore, though; he just turned four a few weeks ago. His name is Micah.*

I send the message and attach a picture of Micah along with it for him to see. I check the time at the top of my phone and it's almost four o'clock, which means I get off soon. I lock my phone, and pack up my belongings and wait for everyone to start leaving for the day. As the last person gets on the elevator, I start making my way to Louis's office. I open his door and he's sitting at his desk looking intently at his computer, so intently that he doesn't notice me when I walk in.

"Are you ready to go?" I ask, pulling his eyes away from the screen.

"Sam, I didn't even hear you walk in." I walk over and stand at the corner of his desk.

"Something on that computer must have been distracting you." He quickly logs off the computer and puts a few papers in his bag before standing up. He gives me a smile that seems to have no emotion behind it.

We begin walking to the elevators, and I know I should probably say something.

"Louis, are you okay?"

"Uh, yeah I'm fine. Just a bit tired that's all." He's lying.

Instead of asking any further questions, I just nod my head and smile. We step off the elevator and start our walk to the coffee shop around the corner. I can tell something is bothering him, but what?

Louis POV

I can't believe what I just read only moments ago. I read it over and over in my head. It can't be true, right? She would tell me, wouldn't she?

Truth

Louis POV

I pushed past a group of drunken people near the front entrance, in hopes to find the person I've been looking all night for. I gripped my phone tightly in my hand, and all I kept thinking about was the text message I read only hours ago. 'I can't do this anymore'. That's it. That was all it took to shred my heart into a million pieces, was those five words.

What couldn't she do anymore? I thought she loved me, and I know there was no doubt that I loved her even more. Last weekend was the best night of my life; we shared something so special together. I thought I actually meant something to her. But now here I am, looking like an idiot at this party, in search of a girl I'm not even sure cares anymore. After checking the next room and finding nothing but another drunken couple making their way to third base, I finally break. I didn't want to give up searching, but I had to. There was no other way I could move on.

"You're so sexy, let's go upstairs!" I'm pulled by my arm by a small blonde girl who

is obviously drunk. I try to escape from her grip and make my way to the door when I bump into a huge crowd and her drunken lips find mine.

"I'm sorry, I have to go." I quickly push the girl off of me and make my way out the door and find my car. I scramble for the keys in my pocket and quickly get in before I can let anyone see me break into tears.

What did I do wrong?

"Are you ready to go?" I'm pulled away from the screen I was just previously focusing on and it took me a second to realize who was speaking.

"Sam, I didn't even hear you walk in." I shuffle some things on my desk and quickly shut the computer off.

"Something on that computer must have been distracting you," I don't say anything, while I reach for some papers to take with me tonight.

"Louis, are you okay?" She asks with a worried expression across her face. How could I lie to such a beautiful face, this girl in front of me is my whole world and more. But she lied to you, Louis.

"Uh, yeah I'm fine. Just a bit tired that's all."

One week ago
"Hello?"

71

"Hi, is this Mr. Melville?" A perky voice echoes through the phone.

"This is him," I log off my computer and carry a few folders with me as I walk to the elevator to leave.

"My name's Kaila and I work here at the hospital. We were wondering if you could come in Monday for a follow up on your son."

"I think you have the wrong number, I don't have a son."

"Louis Melville - that isn't you, sir? Our records show you're a relation to the patient. We need to see Micah on Monday; some of his test results came back."

"Oh, Micah isn't my son. My friend, Samantha, his mother, must have put me down as a reference or emergency contact." I unlock my car and quickly get into the driver's seat, holding the phone between my ear and shoulder while I put the papers in the front seat.

"Micah S. Melville - you're sure that's not your son?" Wait. What?!

"Say that again, please, what's his last name?"

"Micah Melville,"

I drop my phone on my lap and quickly hang up. That can't be right, can it? They must have gotten things mixed up, because there's no way that could be true.

Reactions

Louis POV

Subject: Paternity Test Results
From: Dr. Mallow
Louis, yes you are Micah's biological father. The test results came in this morning. If you'd like to stop by my office, and see for yourself, you are more than welcome.

All the times Samantha brought Micah in for checkups she said she didn't want our office to disclose any of his information with you. But now, seeing that you requested it, and a DNA test, which came back positive, I see that you didn't know about this.

Micah is a great kid; and I hope you and Ms. Foreman can resolve the situation in a positive way. Feel free to contact me anytime for any further information.
Ken Mallow

As we are walking to the coffee shop I do my best to hold back my emotions. I don't know exactly how I feel about the whole thing, but right now I'm just pissed and utterly hurt. I want to stop her in her tracks and ask her to her face about it, but I'd rather not make a scene. How could she hold information like that away from me? I never thought she was that type of person, until now.

We order our drinks and find a table in the back to share. Now Louis, just ask her. I look into her eyes as she takes a sip from her coffee. Those, beautiful, brown eyes that melted my heart. Stop it, Louis, ask her already.

"Are you sure you're okay, Louis, you're acting kind of strange?" she speaks up, setting her coffee down next to her.

"If you knew something that you know would hurt my feelings, you'd tell me right?" I haven't even touched my coffee; I'm just staring at her. What if she lies right to my face? She shifts a bit in her chair before answering my question.

"What are you talking about?"

"Am I his father?"

Samantha's POV

"Am I his father?" He looks at me like he has been since we sat down. I can't decipher exactly how he feels but I know it's not good.

"Louis I was-"

"What the hell, Samantha? How could you not tell me and just make me look like an idiot around him?" He's gripping on to the table and his knuckles are turning white.

74

No, no, no. This can't be happening right here in a fucking coffee shop, of all places. I reach for his arm to try getting him to calm down and not raise his voice so loud, and he flinches.

"I was going to tell you, Louis. Please, you have to believe me."

"Believe you? Why the hell should I believe a thing you say?"

He stands up and heads to the entrance of the coffee shop. I sit there for a moment before processing what just happened in the few short minutes since we came in here. I grab his coffee, and mine, and follow behind him. I see him through the glass door. He pulls his hands through his hair and is pacing back and forth. I slowly open the door and his eyes find mine. I look into his eyes and all I see is Micah. I push the door open, and join him outside.

"Why? That's all I want to know - why would you keep this from me, Samantha? Does he even know that I'm his father?!" I keep my eyes on his and slowly shake my head.

"Louis, I'm so sorry. I wanted to tell you after we started hanging out more. I knew I couldn't hold it in anymore; I wanted to tell you that one night with Zach. I'm sorry, Louis." I reach for his hand and pull it to my heart. "I love you. I never stopped loving you, Louis."

"No, you can't do this to me, Sam. You can't just tell me you love me after something like this. I need time - time away from you. Time to think about all of this. About us, or if there even is an us." He drops his hand from mine and just stands there for a second before his phone rings and breaks our contact.

Or if there even is an us.

What does he mean if? He's not just going to leave me - he wouldn't. Would he? Not after knowing he's a dad. Oh my god, Micah, no he couldn't live without knowing he has a dad and that he's even met him.

"I have to go. I just got a call from my landlord, and he said my rent didn't get to him on time this month, so they're evicting me. Could you fucking believe that? My day is just getting better, and better." He starts walking to where his car is parked, just in front of mine by our building.

"You're always welcome to stay with us until you find a place," I tell him cautiously. He whips his head around and I realize that might not have been such a great idea.

"You're not serious; I just told you I need to be away from you right now, Samantha. We will have our thing at work but we can work that out. I'm just going to go stay with my mom for a few days and figure things out."

"Please don't just push me away Louis. I said I was sorry." He gives me one last glance before opening his car door and mumbling something before getting in.

"Sorry isn't going to cut it this time."

Surprise Doctor

Samantha's POV

So it's been almost a month now since Louis and I have actually talked. After the day at the coffee shop, he called me at two o'clock in the morning. He said he needed to talk to me, to be able to distance himself from our relationship. Ever since that 45 minute phone call we haven't talked since; a few glances at work, but that's all. Micah really misses him, he asked about him a lot at first, but now he doesn't really say much. I feel worse for Micah, than myself - he was so close to Louis, and all along he never even knew that Louis was his dad. I wonder if that's the reason they bonded so quickly when Louis and I started seeing each other.

"Mom, did you know there are only five more weeks until Christmas?"

"No, I didn't buddy. You know what that means, right?" I ask, looking back at him through the rear view mirror of the car.

"Santa is watching me extra close now, making sure I'm a good boy." He smiles while playing with one of his action figures.

"That's right, and it also means you get to go see one of his helpers soon and give him your wish list to bring to Santa." We

pull up to the doctor's office and I unfasten
my seat belt before getting out of the car and
making my way to Micah's door.

"I'm going to ask him for a toy truck and
some money," he tells me after I unbuckle
him from his seat. I take his hand in mine
and we walk into the warm office. I sign
Micah in and we walk to the waiting room
to take a seat.

"Why are you going to ask him for
money?" He plops onto the ground next to
me and grabs a few toys nearby for himself.

"So I can help you pay for the doctor,
and my ears." I almost begin to cry after
hearing his response. I watch him play with
his toys and enjoy this moment with him. I
look up and see someone walk in with a
jacket over his head, shielding them from
the rain that must have begun. The
receptionist points to the person and I see
who it is.

"What are you doing here?" I ask, once
he sits down next to me. Micah gets up off
the floor and recognizes the person who just
sat down next to me.

"Louis!" He yells and quickly crawls
onto his lap. Louis smiles and holds Micah
while he tucks his head into his shoulder.

"You really missed me, didn't you,
buddy?" Micah nods his head and wraps his
arm around Louis.

"Micah?" A female voice asks from the door, I quickly stand up and grab Micah from Louis's lap. He follows me through the door and into the room where the lady asked us to wait for the doctor.

A knock is heard on the door and Dr. Mallow walks through and smiles at the sight of the three of us. Maybe he was the one who asked Louis to come here today. But, why? After checking Micah's heart beat and checking his ears and throat, he decides to take him back for a routine hearing test, leaving Louis and I in the room for a few minutes.

"Why are you here?" I ask him sternly, after Micah leaves with the nurse and Dr. Mallow.

"Dr. Mallow recommended that I come today. He was the one who told me everything."

"What do you mean he told you everything?"

"I got a phone call from here and they told me I needed to take Micah in for a checkup. She told me he was my son and I, for sure, thought they got things mixed up. But apparently not." He pauses and I can tell he's trying to hold back tears. "I called Dr. Mallow the next day and came in for a paternity test. The day we went for coffee was when I found out. The test came back positive."

"Oh," was all I could manage to say while I processed his story in my head. "I really did want to tell you, Louis. I wanted to once I found out, but hearing everything people were saying about me back then, and what they told me about you. And then that night when we were at dinner, I wanted to tell you because I didn't want this secret held back from you any longer."

"I'm starting to accept it now, and I'm glad this happened when it did. I've been talking to Ken a lot, too. He caught me up on Micah's condition and how I could help. I still think we should be friends, Sam, but I'm not sure if I'm ready for a relationship, yet. And I would really like to introduce myself to Micah as his father."

"No, no way. You can't just tell him in an everyday conversation. You could scare him, Louis. You have no idea how he'd react."

"What have you told him about his dad?" He looks at me, and I swear he could burn a hole right through me with his eyes right now.

"Nothing. I mean he knows he has a father but he doesn't ask much about the subject." I think back to the first time Micah asked anything about his dad.

"Mama, where is my dad?" I picked him up from daycare early for a doctor's appointment and he was sitting in the back seat kicking his feet with the cutest smile on his face. He asked me this, like it was something normal to ask - and I guess to him, it was.

"Why do you ask that, buddy?" I don't want to be that mom who tells her kid everything horrible about the dad.

"Daniel asked me why my dad doesn't pick me up from daycare." I think about my response for a second before pulling into the parking lot and turning to face him in the back.

"Your dad is an awesome guy, buddy, and I know that wherever he is I'm sure he loves you very much." He smiles that cute smile, I adore, the same smile as a certain someone I remember from long ago.

"Mom, look I got another sticker for being a good listener during the test again!" Micah bursts through the door with Dr. Mallow soon following in from behind.

"That's so awesome, buddy, why don't you show Louis and maybe he can take you to see Ms. Susan at the front desk for a special treat." He bursts with excitement.

Louis looks at me before picking Micah up and exiting the room.

"So how did everything go?" I ask impatiently. I don't want to leave Micah with him for too long, fearing what Louis could say to him.

"Good. His hearing is still about the same as the last visit. You guys are still going to the signing class, correct?" I nod and he writes something down on a piece of paper, before tearing it off, and handing it to me.

"There is a different place I'd like you to check out. Maybe you could drag Louis along with you, as well; the class is actually for the whole family." Wait. Hold on.

"Ken... Dr. Mallow, I mean. Yes, Louis is Micah's father, but that doesn't mean he can just start popping up like this and going to take classes with us."

"Samantha, I know everything is rough right now for you, but just think about Micah. How much better off he'd be if he knew he had a father. I personally believe Louis would be a great father and role model for him."

"You don't know anything. Micah and I have been fine this far without him. There was a reason why I didn't tell him - it wasn't fair, to him or me, for you to just tell him like you did." I quickly wipe the tears from my face and grab my bag next to me, and walk out of the room. Louis sees me come out and he picks Micah up from where they were sitting.

"Hey buddy, Dr. Mallow said you had a good appointment. Are you ready to go?" He shakes his head and tucks his face into Louis's shoulder again.

"Louis said we could get ice cream." Louis looks like he's about to say something, but I interrupt.

"That's a great idea, buddy. Should we go to the one over by mommy's work, or the one by our house?" He tilts his head, thinking about the decision to make.

"Your work!"

Louis POV

I follow behind Samantha as we drive to the ice cream shop. It also happens to be the place I had taken Sam a few times on our dates. We find parking in front of the building and Samantha helps Micah out of his seat before grabbing his hand. Now that I know I'm his father I'm starting to notice little things about him that I see in myself. It's crazy how much he actually looks like me, but he has her eyes. No doubt about that. He reaches his arms out telling me he wants to be picked up; Samantha gets the door while I pull him up onto my shoulders.

"Mom, look how tall I am!" He shouts to her as we look at all the different flavors of ice cream. Micah points to the flavor he wants, which is the same thing Samantha always got when we came here.

"Two Oreo big scoops with extra Oreo, and one peanut butter fudge big scoop," I order for us. Micah wants to watch as she scoops the ice cream and folds the Oreo bits into it. We stand there for a few moments before I hand her the money for the order and she hands us our cones.

"How's your ice cream, buddy?" I ask as he takes a few licks. I find my answer after he gives me a huge smile with his mouth covered in ice cream.

"Thanks, Lou." I nod as she whispers for Micah to use his manners.

"Thank you, Louis!" Micah gives me, yet again, another ice creamed smile.

"Anything for my son-"
Oh shit...

Micah Melville

Samantha's POV

"Anything for my son-" he slips out.

"You have a son?" I give Louis a stern look, telling him to leave the table for a minute. He excuses himself to the restroom while I talk to Micah.

"Buddy, what he meant was. I mean when he said that, he was talking about you." He looks really confused for a second and I can see that he's trying to understand what I just told him.

This was never my plan; I hoped Micah would have been older so I could explain it all to him. How are you supposed to explain to a four year old that his dad has magically popped back into our lives. I never wanted this to happen, and if Louis had just not applied for the job at my work we would have been fine, and would have never met up again. I hate stupid Ken, too - why decide to tell Louis now?

I look at the clock sitting on the table next to my bed and it reads 4:25 in bright red numbers. I quickly get up and run to the bathroom and I'm soaked. I think my water broke. I quickly change into the pair of sweats I was planning on taking with me when this happened; I grab the diaper bag underneath my bed and shove a few clothes in. I run upstairs and knock quickly on my dad's bedroom door.

"Samantha, is everything okay?" Sophie asks after quickly wrapping her robe around herself.

"I think I'm going into labor." Sophie runs back into the room and wakes my dad up. They both change really quickly and my dad ends up driving me to the hospital, while Sophie stays at home with Kyle.

"I remember when this happened to your mother. She woke me up and told me she was having contractions. It was three in the morning and I had only gone to bed a few hours before that." We pull into the labor and delivery parking lot of the hospital and my dad forces me to get into the wheel chair. He runs me inside and I tell them all my information. They call Dr. Mallow and have him come in to deliver the baby. They take me to the delivery room and connect me to all sorts of machines to track how far my contractions are apart and how the baby is doing.

The sun began to shine through the curtains of our room, and my dad was asleep on the couch. Sophie sent me a text *saying she was on her way over after dropping Kyle off at school for the day. Dr. Mallow told me in a couple hours I should be ready to start pushing. It's almost 8:30 now. Sophie comes into the room and has a McDonalds breakfast in hand and a coffee for my dad.*

"How are things going?" She asks while passing me some food.

"Pretty good. Everything just really hurts right now. This little guy just can't wait to get out." Dr. Mallow also delivered my brother, Kyle. So he's a pretty good friend of the family, and a great doctor.

"So have you decided which last name you'll be giving him, yet?" She cautiously asks.

I've been thinking about it for a while now. I told Sophie everything about Louis when we were still together, and I also told her when we had sex together, back on our anniversary. After I found out I was pregnant she talked to me about a lot of things, most importantly if I wanted to give him his dad's last name. I hated the idea when she first brought it up, because I hated Louis after what happened. But now I'm starting to think it might not be such a bad idea.

"I think Micah Melville has a good ring to it." She smiles, and asks me again if I'm

sure that's what I want. I nod my head and
mentally tell myself it's going to be great.

A few hours later, after almost three
hours of pushing, my miracle came. At
exactly 1:30pm, on July 28th 2010, my
bundle of joy was brought into this world.
Micah Skylar Melville.

"You mean, Louis wants to be my dad?"
He quizzically asks.

"Micah, he is your dad. I didn't want to
tell you like this, buddy, but don't you think
he'd make a good daddy?" He plops his ice
cream cone down on the table and crawls
onto my lap and puts his little head on my
shoulder. This is exactly what I feared, I
didn't want Micah to feel hurt like this, but if
to him this is a way of coping then so be it. I
hold him in my arms and Louis slowly sits
back down, across from us.

"Maybe you should go; I think we need
time to talk." I tell him.

"We can talk together, can't we?" He
looks at Micah crying in my chest and I can
see how hurt he is as well. We decide,
together, that we both need to sit and talk
with Micah, and he can ask all the questions
he might have. We drive back to my place
and Louis follows us.

"Mama, why didn't you tell me he was my dad?" He sniffles in the back seat as we sit at a red light.

"I didn't want you to find out the way you did, buddy. I wanted to wait until you were older, so you'd understand better."

"Does he love me?" I forgot I told him that once.

Your dad is an awesome guy, buddy, and I know that wherever he is I'm sure he loves you very much.

"Yeah, he loves you almost as much as I do." He laughs, and it triggers a laugh from me as well.

"Nobody could love me more than you do, Mama."

"You've got that right, buddy. I love you so much, Micah." When we get home, I get him out of his car seat and lift him into my arms.

Family Reunions

Louis POV

We enter the house and I follow Samantha downstairs to their part of the house. She's carrying Micah, so she sets him down once we enter her bedroom.

"Are your parents here?" I ask her.

"I don't think so. My dad said they were going to meet with some of their friends that were in town for the weekend. I think Kyle might be upstairs. Would you mind watching Micah for a second while I go check?"

"Yeah, of course. Do you think I could get some water, maybe?" She nods her head and kisses Micah on the head before going back upstairs.

Micah gets up off the bed and walks over to his mom's TV and turns it on, grabbing the remote as well. Well, this isn't awkward or anything. I hover, standing over the bed while he sits back on the bed and flicks through the channels before landing on a kids network. He watches for a little while before turning his head back to me. He pats the seat on the bed next to him and I slowly walk over and plop down next to him. Surprisingly, he lays his head on my shoulder and we watch the show for a while before Sam comes back down with two water bottles in hand and a juice box which I assume is for Micah.

"What are you boys doing?" I look down at Micah and he just points to the TV. She laughs and takes a seat at the other side of the bed passing us our drinks.

"Hey, sweetie." Micah turns his head in her direction. "How about we turn the TV off for a bit and we could all talk?"

"Okay, Mama." He makes his way back to the TV and shuts it off and sets the remote down.

"You want to come sit with Mommy?" He climbs on the bed again and lays down in her lap.

"So Louis and I would like to talk to you buddy," she pauses and looks up at me before finishing. "If you have any questions for us, we will try our best to answer them."

The rest of the night consists of Micah asking Samantha and I question after question. Yes, some were kind of silly, but I mean he's four. Samantha was always really good with kids; I was just good at making them laugh sometimes. I check my phone and see that it's almost 8 o'clock, I'm sure it's past Micah's bed time. My thoughts are correct as he yawns and lays his head on

Samantha's shoulder. She lifts him up and carries him to his room, I decide to follow her and stand in the doorway of his room. She pulls his pajama shirt over his head and he laughs as she tickles him at the same time. It's really a sight to see - this is how I pictured our life together.

"Goodnight, Louis," he says as she tucks him into his bed.

"Night Micah, I love you." Before shutting his eyes Samantha places a kiss on his forehead and he smiles.

"I love you, too." I hear him say, and my heart feels like it's growing inside my chest.

Pizza

Samantha's POV

I turn Micah's light off and walk back to my room behind Louis. He sits on the end of my bed awkwardly and I sit back down next to Micah. I thought our conversation went pretty well - Micah asked us a lot of questions; and we gave him the best answers we could.

"So was his appointment good?" He asks, quickly glancing his head up towards me.

"Umm, yeah. He said his hearing is the same as his last visit," I pull out the piece of paper I shoved into my bag next to my bed. I hand it to Louis and he looks at me after looking it over. "He said it would be a good class for the three of us to take."

"Don't you think it's a little, you know, soon?" I shrug my shoulders, I honestly don't know right now.

"I think we should try it. I mean, it really wouldn't hurt, would it? Plus I'm sure Micah would like to spend time with the both of us."

"What do you do, exactly? Like do they just teach you how to do sign language and stuff?" I laugh at his question. I guess from an outsider it sounds kind of weird.

"It's called signing. First they teach you the basics like the alphabet and common greetings. Micah and I started that when he was a year old, now we are doing actual conversations." He nods his head and takes in the information.

"I learned the alphabet my first year at college. I just took it as an elective for a quarter. I think it would be pretty awesome to learn, for him." I just nod, not knowing what to respond with. This is so awkward, and I hate it.

Louis POV

We sit there for a few moments and neither of us says anything. Normally this wouldn't be awkward, but in our situation, it couldn't get any weirder. It's been over a month since we talked, and since I found out about all this. I needed time to gather myself and figure out what to do. It was the hardest thing to do, to leave her the way I did. I love her so much, I always have and I think I always will. I just needed to hear her voice once more to make sure I could leave, that's why I called her the night after our fight. I had had a few drinks, trying to forget her even for a couple hours, but it was impossible.

"Should we talk about us?" she asks softly.

"I don't know if I can right now, it's all been a bit too much for me to handle, Samantha." She nods and I can clearly see the disappointment in her eyes.

"I understand." She picks up her phone as it vibrates on the bed next to her. "Okay, Soph, thanks for calling. Um... well it's still early. I can just order a pizza for us. Okay, we'll see you later. Love you too." She hangs up the phone and looks to me and then back down to her phone.

"Is everything okay?" I ask her as she is typing on her phone. She looks up at me after setting it down next to her again.

"Yeah, she was just calling to tell me they are going to be home late. I texted Kyle to see what kind of pizza he wants me to order. Do you want to maybe stay for dinner?" She asks hesitantly.

"If that's alright with you, I'd love to." She smiles but it quickly turns into a frown when she looks over at her door. I turn my head around to see a sleepy Micah walking in with his blanket trailing behind him.

"Buddy what are you doing?" She asks him, as he climbs next to her on the bed. She cradles him in her arms and kisses him on his forehead.

"I couldn't sleep, and my tummy hurts." He says to her and she takes his hand and kisses it. She's such a good mom. I always knew she would be one day.

"Well, we're going to order some pizza, do you want to stay up and eat with us?" He nods his head and she gets up and walks into the bathroom. She comes back with two pink chewable pills for his upset stomach, I assume.

"I bet if you asked Louis to put a movie on for you, he would." She smiles at me and he sits and thinks about it for a few moments before quickly nodding his head yes.

"Can we watch *Toy Story*?" he asks quietly. I get up after Sam tells me where the movie is and set it in the DVD player next to the TV.

Samantha's POV

Louis hits play and the movie begins. Micah asks him to sit next to him on the bed, after telling him its fine he obliges and Micah moves to his lap. It's a beautiful sight really. I used to always imagine a moment like this, I had little hope that I'd get to see it. I tell Louis I'm going to go upstairs and call in our pizza order.

"Hi, I'd like to place an order for delivery. Yeah, my address is 361 Caters Point. I'd like three large pizzas: One pepperoni with extra cheese, one Hawaiian, and a supreme. And can I get a liter of Pepsi and a root beer? That should be everything. Okay, thank you."

I walk to Kyle's room and take a seat on his bed. He doesn't notice me, being distracted by his video game. I get up and take the headset off his head, causing him to turn around in his chair. I laugh as he flips me his middle finger.

"Pizza will be here in half an hour." He gives me a head nod, and turns back to his video game. What is it with boys and their video games?

I head back downstairs; Louis and Micah are still in the same position. I sit next to them on the bed and let them know the pizza will be here soon. I'm sucked into the movie and lose track of the time when there is a knock at the door. I sit up and realize Louis and I somehow drifted closer to each other. His hand slides off my knee as I get out of the bed and walk upstairs.

"Three large pizzas for a Ms. Foreman." I'm confused for a second, wondering how the delivery guy knows my name. That is until he turns around and I recognize the familiar face.

Sleepover

Samantha's POV

"Liam?"

"I thought I recognized this house."
He smiles and hands me the pizzas from the
carrier.

I immediately envelop him in a hug
and nearly knock him over. I haven't seen
Liam since he and I took classes at the
college together, which was so long ago. I
bring him inside so he's not standing out in
the freezing weather.

"I thought you moved out of state?" I
ask him as we walk into the kitchen.

"I did. I graduated last year and
decided to move back here last month. This
is just my night job," he laughs. "I finally
got my English degree and I work at Hill
Crest Elementary."

I listen as he sums up the last few
years of his life, I can't believe it's been that
long. Liam was my only real friend when I
was at the college, we both took night
classes together and I finished a week before
he told me he was moving. We kept in touch
for the first few months but then we just
kind of stopped. He looks at the time and I

forget that he has to go back to work. I give him another hug and my phone number as he gets back into the small delivery car. I wave goodbye as I make my way back into the house.

"Who was that?" Louis startles me as I'm reaching in the cupboard for the plates.

I turn around and see a blank expression across his face as he leans his back against the counter top and crosses his arms over his chest.

"My old friend from college - he delivered our pizzas." I point at the pizzas and he helps me carry the plates and soda downstairs.

"Oh, cool." We eat our pizza and finish the movie.

I wake up and hear soft snores coming from somewhere; I look up and see that my head is on Louis's chest. I don't even remember falling asleep. Micah is curled up next to me, so I can't really move. I turn my head to look at the clock and its 5:56 in the morning. I lay my head back down and slowly drift back off to sleep, that's when I feel something on the top of my head. He kissed my forehead, most likely thinking I was still asleep. That's when everything else left my mind. All I could think about was Louis, and how much I loved him.

Starting Over

Louis POV

As the movie was playing the credits, I heard soft snores coming from Samantha who was lying beside me with Micah curled up next to her body. I take in the sight for a few minutes before I reach for the remote on the night stand and shut off the TV. As I'm thinking about getting up and leaving for the night, I'm stopped as Samantha moves around and lays her head on my shoulder. I gently run my fingers through her hair and lay my head back, closing my eyes.

"Mama?" I'm awakened by the sound of a hushed voice and I open my eyes to see Micah sitting up trying to wake Samantha.

"Morning, buddy." I say and he smiles.

"Louis, I'm hungry." I nod my head and gently lift Sam off my chest and lay her head down on the pillow. I reach for Micah's hand and we walk upstairs.

"What does your mom usually make you for breakfast, bud?" I lift him up and sit him on the counter top.

"Pancakes!" He shouts. I laugh and look around in the cupboards for pancake mix. I find it and read the back of the package for directions, and then look around again for a mixing bowl and a frying pan. I mix the batter together with water and turn the stove to medium, making sure to follow the directions. I use a measuring cup and put the first scoop on the hot pan, with some spattering off the side. I earn a laugh from Micah and he asks if he can help me flip them over. I hand him the spatula and hold him up by the stove and he flips it over perfectly. I give him a high five as I sit him on the counter again.

We finish the last one together and Micah volunteers to help me get the plates to the table. I made sure to make a few extra pancakes in case her parents or brother want some. As I set the pancakes at the table, a sleepy Sam walks up the stairs causing Micah to run and envelop her in a hug.

"Mama. Louis and I made pancakes!" She picks him up and walks to the table.

"You guys did?" He nods his head and points to the pile of pancakes. "I bet you were an awesome helper." He nods his head again and climbs into his seat.

"How long have you guys been awake?" She asks.

"We woke up about an hour ago." I grab a pancake and put it on my plate; drizzling a load of syrup on it.

"Morning!" I turn around to see Mr. Foreman walk into the dining room with Mrs. Foreman following behind.

"Oh, hi, Louis. I didn't know you were here." She sweetly says, and I can see her drift her eyes in Samantha's direction.

"Uh yeah, I fell asleep last night. I'm sorry,"

"No need to be sorry, any friend of Samantha's is always welcome here." I decide not to say anything further and just nod my head and smile.

"That was a lovely breakfast. Thanks, Louis." She kindly says as she and Sam begin cleaning up the dishes on the table.

"I couldn't have done it without this little helper," I say, as I bounce Micah on my knee. He laughs causing smiles from everyone.

Samantha's POV

I finish putting on Micah's shoes and socks, before letting him go back upstairs to watch TV with Louis and my brother. I pick out a pair of skinny jeans and a simple gray t shirt; I lay it on my bed and walk into the

104

bathroom. I strip out of my clothes and immerse myself under the hot water.

I couldn't stop thinking about Louis while I was standing under the fall of water. Everything that's happened in just a few short weeks seems so unreal - he actually knows now - and he's accepting it! I used to think when he'd run from the situation when he found out, and not be in Micah's life. I'm glad he stayed, and I'm even happier that he wants to be more involved in our lives. I owe him that much, after keeping such a huge secret from him for so many years.

I wrap my towel around myself and walk back into my room, I'm startled after I pull my jeans over my waist. I'm standing there shirtless and Louis just walked into the room with an obvious mortified look on his face.

"Oh shit, I'm sorry." He says before turning around quickly.

"It's nothing you've never seen before." I laugh, trying to ease the tension that's obvious in the room. He turns back around to face me and his mouth curls into a smile.

"So, you guys are leaving?" He asks while walking over and sitting on the edge of the bed.

"Yeah. Micah has a play date with my friend's daughter." He nods and runs his fingers through his hair. "You could come if you want; I know her fiancé will be there, too. We're just going to the park and probably for some coffee or something."

"Would I have time to run to my place and change really quick?" I look at the time on my phone and nod my head.

"Yeah, we could pick you up on our way if you want?" We plan to meet up at his place to pick him up in half an hour.

I walk back upstairs and plop myself down on the couch with my brother and Micah. We watch TV for a few more minutes before I decide we should get ready to leave. I pull out my phone and dial Kaila's number.

"Hey!" She answers.

"Hey, I just wanted to let you know Micah and I are just getting ready to leave." I pull my seatbelt over myself and click it in place.

"Okay, Eric is driving through McDonald's right now. We should be there around the same time as you two."

"Actually, about that…" I pause for a second, "Louis is coming with us." The phone goes quiet for a second before she answers.

"Oh my god, does he know?" She quietly asks, and I laugh.

"Yeah, it's a long story. I'll tell you later. I'm picking him up now, so I'll see you guys in a little bit." I hang up the phone and send Louis a quick text letting him know I'm here.

Play Date

Samantha's POV

We pull into the parking lot in front of the huge park. Surprisingly, it's not very busy - it must be the cold autumn weather. Micah and I don't mind it at all, though. Louis and I get out of the car and he helps Micah get out from the back seat and he lifts him up, plopping him onto his shoulders.

"Kaila said they should be here shortly - they were getting lunch when I called." We sit on a bench close to where the swing set is and Micah runs off to play.

Just as he runs off, I see a familiar car pull up next to mine and see that it's Eric and Kaila. Louis chases after Micah, leaving me on the bench by myself.

"Hey," I greet them both and Kaila sits down next to me while Eric carries their daughter Arielle to the swings.

"So where is he?" she asks.

"He and Micah ran off somewhere." I point in the direction where Micah ran off with Louis. "There they are - he's going down the slide."

"Ooh, he's tall and hot." She adds.

I playfully hit her shoulder and we both laugh. I do have to admit, Louis is very attractive. In high school all the girls really liked him.

"How did he find out?"

"Long story, but basically Dr. Mallow spilled the beans. Someone called Louis from his office and that's how he initially found out. I was planning on telling him, I just wasn't sure how." I shrug my shoulders and she gives me a hug.

"Well let's hope he'll get his shit together and be a good dad for Micah." I nod and look up to see Louis and Micah walking back alongside Eric and Arielle.

"Louis, this is my friend Kaila. Kaila, this is Louis." They shake hands and I see he and Eric already did introductions with each other.

Micah and Arielle run off together, hand in hand, and head for the big slide and the monkey bars. The four of us take a seat at a nearby table so we can all talk.

"So Louis, what do you do for a living?" Eric asks politely.

"Oh, I'm the manager at Morises. I actually work in the same division as Samantha, that's how we ran into each other."

"You guys knew each other before?" he asks. Louis just nods his head.

"We used to date in high school," I tell Eric. "That's when I got pregnant."

Well that was a conversation stopper. He coughs a little before politely speaking up; and breaking the silence.

"How about we go check on the kids?" He asks Kaila.

She turns her head towards me and I just nod my head, knowing they probably want to leave Louis and me alone for a few minutes. They both get up and start walking to the playground where Micah and Arielle are playing together.

"I'm sorry." He looks down at his feet, and I can't really tell what he's thinking

"There's no need to be sorry, Sam. You need to stop apologizing so much. I was the one who left, when you needed me the most. I can understand, now, why you would want to keep something like that away from me. I'm not saying it was right, but I do understand." I run my fingers through his beautiful brown hair and pull his face closer to mine.

"I love you. I don't want to worry about the past anymore, because all we have is right now. And right now all I want is your lips pressed against mine."

His hands find their way into my hair and he crashes his lips with mine. I'm pulled into a universe where it's just the two of us - in this moment - for what feels like forever. I turn around to see Eric and Kaila standing with the kids and they're all clapping their hands, as if they knew this was bound to happen. Louis wraps his fingers around my own and kisses the top of my head as we walk towards the playground.

Made in the USA
San Bernardino, CA
27 April 2016